SUPERDOG
THE HERO

8
9
1 8
2 7
3 6
4 5
5 4
6 3
7 2
8 1
9 0

By the same author

SUPERDOG
SUPERDOG IN TROUBLE

SUPERDOG
THE HERO

David Henry Wilson

Illustrated by Linda Birch

KNIGHT BOOKS
Hodder and Stoughton

First published in Great Britain
in 1986 by Hodder and
Stoughton Limited
Knight Books edition 1992

British Library C.I.P.

Wilson, David Henry
  Superdog the hero
  I. Title II Birch, Linda
  823'.914[J]   PZ7

  ISBN 0 340 58010 0

Printed and bound in Great Britain
for Hodder and Stoughton
Children's Books, a division of
Hodder and Stoughton Ltd., Mill
Road, Dunton Green, Sevenoaks,
Kent TN13 2YA (Editorial Office:
47 Bedford Square, London WC1B
3DP) by Clays Ltd., St. Ives plc.

Contents

I
Forewoof

Everybody's talking about my book. It's a best-seller, and I've had millions and millions of letters. In fact, both of them are on the floor in front of me. One says:

Dear Superdog,
　　Thank you for your last book. It will be your last book, won't it?
　　　　　　　　Yours hopefully,
　　　　　　　　Dog-lover

It's great to receive a thank you straight from the heart. The other letter says:

Dear Superdog,
　　My gerbil loves your book. It tears so easily.
　　　　　　　　Yours gratefully,
　　　　　　　　Gerbil-lover

Obviously my book appeals to all sorts of people and animals, and so here I am again with another collection of my amazing adventures.

Just in case anyone doesn't know who I am, I'd better tell you that I'm Woofer, better known as Superdog. It wouldn't be modest of me to tell you all my super-qualities, but I'll tell you some of them. I'm incredibly handsome, strong, fast, intelligent, brave . . . well, I can't think of any more for the moment, but you'll see just why I'm called Superdog when you read on.

I live with the Brown family. Mr Brown can never make up his mind, so Mrs Brown always makes it up for him. Mrs Brown always knows what she wants, and what she usually wants is for me to have a bath. I get on very well with both of them – a Superdog gets on well with everybody – but I don't always get on as well with them as when I do get on well with them, if you see what I mean.

I always get on well with Tony and Tina.

They're Mr and Mrs Brown's children. They're a lot more intelligent than Mr and Mrs Brown because they understand me, and because I understand them. I don't always understand Mr and Mrs Brown. For instance, I don't understand why Mr Brown says he'll do something but doesn't do it. Mrs Brown always does what she says she'll do, and what I can't understand is why she wants to do it in the first place.

There are some other important characters I must mention. Honey . . . . Oh, sorry about that. I went off in a little day-dream then. I'm always dreaming about Honey. She's the lady dog who lives four doors away. Can you picture a tin of liver and onions? Well, Honey is *ten times more beautiful*.

And she's a thousand times more beautiful than the black and white tom-cat that lives next door. That cat is an evil monster. I shan't say any more about him, because it would put you off. Anyway, you'll see for yourself what he's like.

I think that's enough introduction now, so I'll get on with the stories. I hope you'll enjoy them. I do.

2
The Bone

Bones. Ah, show me a bone and I'll show you a happy dog. I don't, of course, mean those awful rubber bones that are an insult to a dog's brain and taste-buds – no, I mean the real thing, juicy, crunchy, crackly, marrowy bones.

I'm going to tell you a story about a bone, but I'd better warn you that it's a sad story. Not everybody likes sad stories, and this story is sadder than most sad stories because it happened to me. Even today the thought of it brings tears to my eyes, though it happened a long time ago.

A leg of lamb, that was the bone in question. The family had been sitting round the dinner-table, munching meatily, and I'd put on my starved expression, letting out the occasional hollow whine to attract their attention.

'Here we are, boy,' said Mr Brown, holding out a rich fatty slice.

I bounded towards him with astonishing speed for a starving dog, but even that astonishing speed was not speedy enough.

'Maybe not,' he said, whisking the treasure away just before I could get my teeth into it. 'Might make a mess on the carpet.'

'Anyway, you shouldn't encourage him,' said Mrs Brown. 'Let him eat at the proper time and the proper place.'

As far as I am concerned, the proper time and the proper place have always been here and now, but Mrs Brown has fixed ideas on such matters, and no dog on earth could unfix them for her. I uttered my heartbroken whimper, and drooped my way round to the children's side of the table.

'Poor Woofer,' said Tina, and accidentally dropped a piece of meat for me. I think Tina's my favourite member of the Brown family.

'Poor old Woofer,' said Tony, and was also about to let me have a taste when Mrs Brown stopped him.

'No, Tony,' she said. 'Woofer will have his later.'

Tony's my second favourite, and Mrs Brown is my last favourite. But when the Browns had finished making pigs of themselves (if you can make a pig of yourself eating lamb), and as I lay on the carpet too weak to move, Mrs Brown suddenly rose to her feet with some of the sweetest words she'd ever spoken:

'Come on, Woofer, it's your turn now.'

The sound of her voice brought new strength to my legs, and I followed her into the kitchen almost tripping over my own tongue. And there in the kitchen I received The Bone. *What* a bone! I practically dislocated my jaw trying to pick it up. It was huge, it was meaty, it was solid, it was weighty, and sweeter-smelling and sweeter-tasting than anything since my famous Christmas Turkey.

'Perhaps you'd better take it outside,' said Mrs Brown.

I would have taken it anywhere. If she'd told me to take it through fire, floods, or even next door's garden, I'd have taken it. She opened the door for me, and I half carried, half dragged my treasure out on to the back lawn, where I gripped and ripped, bounced and pounced, nuzzled and guzzled until I could rip-pounce-guzzle no more.

That, of course, did not mean that I'd finished with the bone. On the contrary, I seemed to have made scarcely any impression on it. There were still weeks and weeks of entertainment left in it, and the great problem facing me now was how to keep it safe till I was ready for another taste of the action. Well, the obvious thing to do was bury it, and so I looked around for a suitable burial place.

Perhaps I should mention that as I looked around, I noticed next door's black and white tom-cat watching me from the roof of their shed. As he was a long way away, was sitting down, and showed no desire to get up, I felt fairly safe. You may wonder, therefore, why I mention him at all, but I have a reason which I will explain later.

Once I had assured myself that the black and white enemy had no intention of attacking me, I resumed my hunt for a bone-hiding place. And the spot I eventually chose was next to a yellow flower which I would have no trouble finding again.

A few lunges of my powerful hind legs, and in no time at all I'd dug a hole deep and wide enough to take my superbone. Tenderly I laid it to rest, and then scraped the earth back over it. With one last look I trotted back to the house, well satisfied with a good day's work.

I didn't forget my bone. How could anyone forget a bone like that? Even now I haven't forgotten it, after all these years, so I certainly didn't forget it after just a few days. But for various reasons – mainly connected with Mrs Brown's excellent cooking and/or choice of dog foods – I didn't actually feel the urge to go boning until a week or two had gone by. But when the urge did come, out I went into the garden with that same feeling of intense yumyum that I had had on following Mrs Brown into the kitchen.

The first shock that I had was that my yellow flower had disappeared. It was still there, of course, but had disappeared among hundreds and hundreds of similar yellow flowers, and I'm afraid one yellow flower smells just like another yellow flower. And so there I stood with my head full of lamb's leg and my nose full of yellow. There was nothing I could do except make a guess and dig. So I guessed and dug. A couple of quick leg-lunges were enough to prove that I'd guessed wrong, and so I moved on. The next guess proved as boneless as the first.

It was all the fault of the flowers. If they hadn't spread themselves everywhere, and if they hadn't equipped themselves with this all-covering pong, I'd have had no trouble. Or that was what I thought at the time. I therefore had two good reasons for getting rid of them: one, to clear the way to my beloved bone, wherever it was; and two, revenge. So I took my revenge, and I cleared the way. Even at that age, my superstrength was too much for those yellowsmellers. I clawed them out faster than a wasp can flap its wings, and even the toughest of them soon found itself flying through

the air at the touch of my hind leg.

'What do you think you're doing!' came a piercing shriek, and across the lawn raced Mrs Brown, with her face as white as a bone. 'You bad dog, you naughty dog, you wicked dog!'

Even though she was looking at me and coming at me, I could hardly believe that she was really talking to me. What was bad, naughty, or wicked about young Woofer?

Thump! That was her hand making contact with my bottom. Well, I didn't wait to argue with her, but set out across the lawn, trying to put as much grass, air and space as possible between her hand and my bottom. On the way, I just happened to glance up in the direction of next door's shed, and there on the roof sat that evil black and white tom-cat. I'll swear he was smiling, and if I hadn't been in such a hurry I might well have stopped to ask him what he was smiling at. On the other hand, I might not – he can be a bit frightening, that cat.

'What's the matter, Mummy?' asked Tina, hopping across the garden.

'It's Woofer!' cried Mrs Brown. 'He's ruined all my lovely daffs!'

'Oh Woofer, you naughty boy,' said Tina.

I sat on the grass and let out a whimpery

whine to tell her that I was not a naughty boy but a sadly deboned and unjustly thumped dog.

'I expect he was looking for something,' said Tina, who always understands me.

'Well, he'll find a slap on the bottom and no supper,' said Mrs Brown, who never understands anything. Then she got down on her hands and knees, and do you know what she did? She actually started putting those yellow nuisances back in the ground! She did! She was picking them up, digging little holes, sticking the flowers in, patting earth all around them . . . undoing all the good work that I'd just done! It was enough to make even the toughest dog howl. And howl I most certainly did. I would have gone on howling if Mrs Brown hadn't shouted at me to keep quiet.

The bone was never found. I count that as one of the most tragic events of my life. From time to time I still go to that patch of ground (when it's free of yellow-smellers) to have a quick scrape and sniff. But there's never been even a splinter of bone or a whiff of lamb. It seems incredible that such a priceless treasure should vanish completely and for ever, yet that is what has happened. Unless, of course, there is a plain straightforward explanation. I have often wondered what it was that my hated enemy the tom-cat was smiling about that day. Could it be that cats . . .? But no, cats don't eat bones, do they? Or do they?

3
The Header

This adventure began in our back garden and ended in the park, and I remember the beginning much better than the end. What I remember most about the end is that it was very painful, so I think I'd prefer to talk about the beginning.

Mr Brown, Tony and I were in the back garden. It was a fine spring day, and we were playing football on the lawn. Mr Brown and Tony were trying to kick the ball to each other, and I was trying to kick the ball to myself. I am, of course, quite brilliant at sport, which I suppose is due to my superspeed and superstrength. Give me a ball, and I'll show you a dozen tricks you never thought of. It's true that I did have a bit of trouble controlling the football, but that was because it kept rolling away from

me. If it hadn't been so round and rolly, I'd have had no trouble at all.

'Leave it, Woofer!' Mr Brown kept crying. I didn't need to leave it. It was leaving me.

'Here, boy!' cried Tony. And I would have kicked it to him if it had stayed still enough for me to kick it.

We'd been playing for some time when Mr Brown did a trick that not even I had ever thought of. He threw the ball up in the air, and then let it bounce on his head straight off to Tony. I thought that was rather clever. So did Tony, because he tried to do the same trick, only the ball missed his head and bounced off his shoulder. Naturally, I was eager to try it out for myself, but not even I can manage to throw balls up in the air. Fortunately, Tony guessed what I wanted, so he sent the ball bouncing towards me. With perfect timing, I leapt high and met it square on my forehead. It flew like a frightened cat right across the lawn and swish! crunch! into Mrs Brown's daffodils.

'What a header!' shouted Tony.

'Woofer one, daffodils nil,' said Mr Brown.

From that moment on, we had a brand-new game to play, and great fun it was, too. Except, perhaps, for the daffodils. Even after Mr Brown had gone indoors, Tony stayed to throw the ball to me, and Tina came out to see what all the fuss was about.

'Just look at Woofer heading the ball!' said Tony.

And it really must have been quite a sight. I sent that ball all over the garden, and I reckon we might have gone on all day and all night if Mrs Brown hadn't come out to rescue her flowers.

'All those hours spent planting – not to mention replanting,' she said, 'and you children and Woofer knock them all down in ten minutes.'

Mrs Brown isn't much of a sports fan.

Woofer's headers soon became pretty famous. Mr Brown would take me into the park, and instead of throwing the ball for me to chase, he'd throw it for me to head. People used to crowd round to watch me head the ball. Well, one or two people, anyway. And to tell the truth, I much preferred heading it to picking it up in my mouth. Tennis balls especially have a nasty rubbery flavour, and when you've had a mouthful of that, you start hoping that the next throw will land in a fast-flowing river.

There's a fortune to be made if someone can invent liver-and-onion flavoured tennis balls.

Well, that's the beginning of the story, and I wish it was also the end, but it's not. The big mistake came a few weeks later. Everything started quite normally. Mr Brown said:

'I think I'll take Woofer for a walk this afternoon. Or shall I? Yes, I might as well. Unless we stay at home. No, we'll go for a walk.'

The children decided they'd come, too, then Mr Brown decided that the children could take me and he needn't go, but Mrs Brown said he needed the exercise, and so finally the children and I took Mr Brown off to the park.

We went along the usual route: past Honey's house, where I wanted to stop and have a sniff but got pulled away; past the toy shop, where the children wanted to stop and have a look but got pulled away; and past The Dog and Duck, where Mr Brown wanted to stop and have a drink but pulled himself away.

Everything in fact was quite normal until we reached the park. What was happening in the park was rather strange. There were men in white clothes standing all over the place.

'Ah!' said Mr Brown. 'Cricket!'

It must have been some sort of game, though it was a very peculiar game. Most of the time, none of the men in white clothes did anything at all. They just stood there, or walked up and down. I only knew that it *was* a game because in the distance I saw a ball, which one man in white threw at another man in white, who hit it or missed it with a club.

Mr Brown stood there watching it all as if there were nothing more interesting in the whole wide world. He watched that game like a child watching a bag of sweets, or a grown-up watching television, or me watching Honey. He couldn't take his eyes off it. And Tony, Tina and I, who had come along for some entertainment, stood there waiting for something to happen.

'We may as well sit down while we're standing up,' said Mr Brown, and gently lowered himself on to the grass.

'We want to play,' said Tina.

'We don't want to watch boring old cricket,' said Tony.

'Hear, hear,' said I.

'Well, you can run around if you like,' said Mr Brown. 'But don't go on the field of play.'

'What play?' said Tina.

'You mustn't cross this white line,' said Mr Brown.

He took off my leash, and Tony, Tina and I set to work chasing the ball which they'd brought along. Naturally, I did a few of my famous headers, and there was even some applause from around the park, which must have been for me because nobody could have wanted to clap the cricket.

It's now that we come to the painful bit. Ouch! I can feel it right between the eyes just thinking about it.

We were playing quite happily when suddenly there was a cry of 'Look out!' I turned round, and coming straight out of the sky towards me was the red ball the cricketers had been playing with. Everybody was looking at me, and I knew at once what they wanted me to do. Obviously they'd all got thoroughly bored with their cricket, they'd seen me putting on a fantastic show heading our ball to Tony and Tina, and now they wanted to join in our game.

The ball bounced once, and came towards me at just the right height. If they wanted a show, they'd get a show. I did a tremendous leap high into the air, and met the cricket ball fair and square with my forehead. It must have been the finest header ever seen in the park.

What I didn't know was that a cricket ball is as hard as a can of bone wrapped in concrete. I just had time to hear the crack, feel the crunch, and see ten thousand lights flash before my eyes, and then night fell all over me. The next thing I knew was that I woke up with a crowd of people round me. Someone was saying: 'What a brave dog!' and someone else said: 'He saved that little girl's life.'

Of course it's true that I am a brave dog, but how I can have saved anyone's life by heading a cricket ball, I shall never know. I suppose they were mixing it up with another of my adventures. And as I lay on the grass with my pain between my eyes, I wasn't thinking about how brave I was. I was thinking how headachy I was.

Mind you, everyone must have enjoyed the show, because when Mr Brown picked me up to carry me home, there was a big round of applause from all the cricketers and all the people round the cricket field. I suppose they'd never seen such a super-header before. All the same, I made a promise to myself, and it's a promise I've never broken: that superheader was the last header I ever made. From that moment onwards, the nearest any ball has ever come

to my head is when I chase after one of the Browns' tennis balls, pick it up in my mouth, and carry it back. It may have a nasty rubbery flavour, but I'd sooner have a nasty rubbery flavour in the mouth than a nasty solid cricket ball between the eyes.

4
Sick as a Dog

The moment I woke up, I knew something was wrong. I felt terrible. I tried to raise my head, but it was just as if someone had put a heavy weight on top of it. Well actually in a manner of speaking they had, because it was wedged under the sideboard. But it wasn't the sideboard that was hammering between my eyes. That was coming from inside.

I tried to stand up, but even if the sideboard hadn't knocked me down, my legs wouldn't have carried me. Those superlegs, which could take me such distances at such speeds, had now turned into blobs of marrowbone jelly. And strange things were happening inside my stomach, too. It was gurgling like a bath with the plug taken out.

You might think a Superdog would never

get ill, but with that hammer in my head and bathwater in my stomach, I really didn't care what you might think. The fact is, if a Superdog gets ill, it's no ordinary illness, and I was very worried about myself. I'd have worried myself sick if I hadn't been sick already. Clearly I had to do something, and so I did what any true hero would have done: I lay quite still under the sideboard and groaned.

It was Tina who found me, and she knew straight away that something was wrong. I made sure that she knew, by letting out a very loud whine.

'What's wrong, Woofer?' she asked. 'What are you doing under the sideboard?'

It should have been obvious to her that I was dying under the sideboard, and I told her so in my most dying voice.

'What's the matter?' asked Tony, joining Tina.

'It's Woofer,' said Tina, 'I think he's ill.'

'Woo woo, hammer gurgle, woo woo!' I groaned.

'We'd better tell Mummy,' said Tony.

His feet went pounding up the stairs, and I groaned again.

'Don't worry, Woofer,' said Tina, kneeling beside me, 'Mummy will know what to do.'

Mrs Brown always knew what to do: namely, to put me in the bath. The first thing she says when she sees me is: 'That dog needs a bath.' Anyone would think I was smelly. Anyway, I certainly didn't feel like a bath today. I never do feel like a bath, but I feel even less like a bath when I'm lying under the sideboard dying.

'Woo woo!' I moaned, too weak even to say woof.

Mrs Brown was still in bed. So was Mr Brown. It was normal for Mr Brown to be still in bed, because he was always the last person to get up – usually saying: 'Oh good heavens, is that the time already?' But it wasn't normal for Mrs Brown. She was always the first person to come downstairs – usually poking me in my basket and saying: 'Wake up, Woofer. About time you had your bath.' Anyway, she was still in bed.

It must have been because of the party. There had been a party the night before, with a lot of jolly people making a lot of noise. There was a woman with a laugh rather like my famous woof-howl, and everybody had found that very funny. I thought they might like to hear the real woof-howl, too, but they didn't seem to appreciate that at all, and Mr Brown made me go out of the room.

I don't remember much about the party. Somebody asked Mr and Mrs Brown exactly what they were celebrating, and Mrs Brown answered that it was their twelfth wedding anniversary. Then Mr Brown said he still didn't know what they were celebrating, and everybody laughed. The woof-howl woman laughed loudest, and that was when I did *my* woof-howl and got sent out.

Tony and Tina weren't allowed at the party. They were supposed to be asleep, though to sleep through all that noise they'd have needed to be as deaf as a sideboard. I went up to see them, and played with them for a while. Then Tina went downstairs to ask for a drink of water, and Tony went to ask for a drink of water, too. I went with them to ask for anything I could get, and . . . yes, that was when something rather strange happened. Mrs Brown took them out for their drink of water, and a fat man with a red face and a balloon belly called me over.

'Here, boy!' he said.

I didn't like the look of him, so I pretended not to hear, but he called me again:

'Come on, boy! Come and have a drink with Uncle Toby.'

He had a silly grin on his face, which humans often put on when they think they're being clever. I gave him my maybe-nice-may-be-nasty-dog grunt, and wandered vaguely towards and away from him.

'This way, boy,' he said. 'Drink for the nice doggy.'

All this talk of drink was making my mouth feel very dry. And I've learnt in life that nothing cures a dry mouth better than a wet drink. And so I wandered within drinking reach.

'Here we are, then, boy,' said Toby. 'Wet your woof with this.'

I did. Just a cautious sip to start with, because although I'm the most adventurous creature you'll ever meet, I'm a bit suspicious of things I haven't tried before. It tasted bitter, but it was cold and refreshing and very undry-mouthing.

'He likes it,' said Toby.

I did like it.

'Steady, Woofer,' said Mr Brown.

But it turned out that I was even thirstier than I thought I was. By now they were all crowding round watching me, and as they were enjoying my performance, I carried on performing. Toby poured me another glassful, which I lapped up with no difficulty at all, and everybody clapped, and the woof-howl woman woof-howled. We were all having a marvellous time.

After that I remember doing some special woofs, wuffs and woowoos to keep them entertained, and I tried to do a little dance on my hind legs but fell over and knocked down a vase. I think I knocked over some other things as well, but my memories of the rest of the evening are very fuzzy. I know my legs seemed to have different ideas about where to go, and every time I fell over I thought it was funnier than the time before. But my next really clear memory is of waking up under the sideboard.

'I know what's the matter with him,' said Mrs Brown.

'What?' asked Tina.

'The same as your father,' said Mrs Brown. 'It's a dose of the morning after the night before.'

'What's that?' asked Tony.

'Heart's delight Saturday night,' said Mrs Brown, 'trouble dawning Sunday morning.'

I still didn't know what she was talking about, but when Tina asked if I was going to die, I listened very anxiously to her reply.

'No, he's not going to die,' said Mrs Brown.

If I hadn't been so ill, I would have let out a cheer.

'Can you make him better?' asked Tony.

'I think so,' said Mrs Brown. 'What that dog needs is a bath.'

If I hadn't been so ill I would have let out a howl. Instead, I used my last ounce of strength to push myself back against the wall under the sideboard.

'Help me get him out,' said Mrs Brown.

I uttered a low sad moan, indicating that I was far too ill to be moved, but once Mrs Brown has made up her mind, she never unmakes it. Before long, I was being carried through to the kitchen, as limp and lifeless as an old fur coat.

Oh, the shock of that cold water! The moment it hit me, I leapt to my feet with a howl. But Mrs Brown had no pity. The children held me, and she scrubbed me all over. If this was making me better, then being better was ten times worse than being ill. By the time she'd finished, I was ready to leap out of my tin tub and run a mile. Mind you, the hammering had stopped in my head, the gurgling had stopped in my stomach, and my legs were back to super-strength. But no illness can keep a Super-dog down for long, and there was certainly no need for that sort of treatment.

'Now,' said Mrs Brown, 'we'll see if we can't use the same method on Daddy.'

There are times when I feel quite sorry for Mr Brown.

5
The Kennel

Life is full of surprises. For years Mr Brown had been promising to build me a kennel. And for years he's been putting it off. So what was the surprise? Well, no, he didn't actually build the kennel – that would have been a miracle rather than a surprise – but he did buy one. It was Mrs Brown who spotted the advertisement in the newspaper, told Mr Brown to ring up about it, and made Mr Brown jump into his car and fetch it. But it was Mr Brown who brought it home and set it up in the garden. That was the surprise.

'There you are, Woofer,' he said. 'A little house just for you.'

There was something about the little house that I wasn't too sure about. I jumped up and down, wagged my tail, and said woof several times, as they expected, and then I had a good sniff round. I didn't like what I sniffed. The whole thing smelt of underdog. I know a low-class dog when I smell one, and the dog that had had this kennel before me was as low down as a dog can get.

We dogs have a special way of covering up smells we don't like. I raised my hind leg and did a diddle.

'Woofer!' cried Mrs Brown. 'How could you?'

'Maybe he's christening it,' said Mr Brown.

With underdog smell replaced by super-dog fragrance, the kennel seemed more like home. It was bright and comfortable, with room to sit, stand or lie. Mrs Brown gave me a soft cushion, and I could picture myself on a hot summer's afternoon lying there in the shade, occasionally twitching my tail and watching the world go by. If I happened to be outside and it started to rain, I could quickly pop into my little shelter and listen to the rain pattering on the roof above me. Yes, the kennel was a great idea.

But Mr and Mrs Brown had something else in mind. It was probably Mrs Brown who had it in mind, since Mr Brown's mind very rarely has anything in it. The kennel wasn't just for me to rest or shelter in. She expected me to sleep in it.

Now, ever since I can remember, I've slept in a basket in the hall. I have a special corner all of my own, under the stairs right out of everybody's way, and it's snug and it's cosy and it's mine. Woofer's corner it's called. At least, that's what I call it. That is where I sleep, that is where I've always slept, and that is most certainly where I wanted to continue sleeping. So you can imagine the shock, the horror, the dismay when that night Mrs Brown said to Mr Brown:

'Time for Woofer to go to his kennel.'

At first I thought she'd said 'corner', but no sooner had I set out for the hall than Mr

Brown was taking me by the collar and leading me towards the back door.

'Come on, Woofer,' he said. 'It's the kennel for you.'

'No, no,' I said, 'she meant "corner". I'm not sleeping out there!'

I braced my legs, but he dragged me out into the night.

'Come on, Woofer, you know you like your new kennel.'

Of course I liked it, but not for sleeping in. Woofer's corner was for sleeping in.

I wasn't sure whether to whimper pathetically or howl despairingly, so I sort of whimper-howled and howl-whimpered. This brought Mrs Brown out to investigate.

'What a fuss!' she said. 'Well, he'll soon get used to it.'

'No-o-o-o-o!' I howled.

'I wowowowon't,' I whimpered.

'In you go, Woofer,' said Mr Brown, pushing me in with one hand and shining his torch with the other.

As soon as I was in, I turned round and came out again.

'Woofer!' snapped Mrs Brown in her bath-whether-you-like-it-or-not voice. There was no hope for me once she used that voice. Tony and Tina would have understood and pleaded for me, but they were both fast asleep in bed. In their bedrooms. In the house. Where they ought to be. Where *I* ought to be.

'Owowowowow!' I howled.

'Stop that!' said Mrs Brown.

'Maybe he should get used to the kennel before we make him sleep in it,' suggested Mr Brown.

I thought that was quite a good suggestion.

'The only way he'll get used to it,' said Mrs Brown, 'is by being in it.'

Then do you know what she did? She tied me to the kennel. She actually tied me to it so that I couldn't get away. Me – innocent, loving, harmless, good-natured Woofer – tied up and left alone in the dark, while the rest of the family stayed safe and secure inside the house. What had I done to deserve this? What was going to be done to *me*? Who could tell what terrible things might happen to a dog left alone in the dark?

I don't want you to think that I was actually afraid. Superdogs don't know the meaning of fear, and anyone who has followed my life-story will know that courage is one quality I have plenty of. No, the feeling that I had certainly wasn't fear. Not ordinary fear, anyway. The problem was that with my superintelligence, and my superimagination, I was able to work out just what it meant to be out there in the night. Not even my remarkable eyes and nose could perceive everything in the sha-dows. A monster could come creeping up on me in the dark, and I wouldn't even know it was there until it was too late.

I let out a little whimper. It was such a sad sound that anyone who heard it would immediately take pity on the whimperer, open the kitchen door, and let him go straight to his snug, safe corner where he belonged. But nobody did hear it.

Then the thought occurred to me that not everybody *would* take pity on the whimperer. A monster, for instance, would be very pleased to hear a whimper like that. I'd better keep quiet and pretend I wasn't there.

I curled up on the floor of my kennel, with my head pressed against the back, and my eyes tightly closed. It's easy to close your eyes. You just get the top bit to fall down till it meets the bottom bit. But how do you close your ears? I have amazing control over all my muscles, but none of my ear muscles was able to get the top bit to fall down to the bottom bit. Every rustle, every whisper, every crack and every creak went straight into my ears and down to my thumping heart. At one time I heard quick and heavy breathing right next to my ear, and it was only when I moved my head that I realised it was me.

Perhaps it wasn't such a good idea to have my head at the back of the kennel. After all, if something *did* come, I ought to be able to see it and howl for help before it got me. Yes, head to the front would give me a better chance.

I stood up, opened my eyes, turned round, and felt my blood run as cold as cold turkey. I would certainly have fallen down if my knees hadn't gone rigid with the shock, and my heart missed half a dozen beats before catching up at greyhound speed. I was gazing into two huge and glaring eyes that blazed at me out of a bristling black shadow. I can't describe how terrifying those eyes were. They were ten times brighter than Mr Brown's torch, and they were ten times fiercer than Mrs Brown's bath-whether-you-like-it-or-not voice. Only the most evil monster in the

world could have eyes like that, and they were burning into mine as if to say 'I'm coming to get you.'

I was saved by my astonishing instincts. Without even stopping to think, I opened my mouth and my lungs and let out a howl such as not even I had ever howled before. It sounded something like: 'Heeeeweeelpo-wowowow!' And having started, I didn't stop. Such was my courage that I didn't even care whether other monsters heard me and came running to attack. I just wanted Mr and Mrs Brown to hear it and to save me.

'Miaow!' said the monster, and the eyes suddenly turned away and I thought I saw its huge black shadow moving off into the night. But I was taking no chances.

'Heeeeweeeelpowowowow!' I howled, and I went on howling until at last the kitchen door opened.

At the same time, a window in the next house was flung open and a voice shouted: 'Will you keep that mongrel of yours quiet!'

Mongrel! That's the house with the black and white tom-cat, which just goes to show what taste they have. Mongrel!

'Sorry, Mr Thomas!' called Mr Brown.

Well, I was so relieved to hear his voice that, to be honest, I didn't even mind being called a mongrel – not then, anyway. But I let out one more 'Heeeeweeeelpowowowow!' just to make sure he didn't leave me.

'That dog's a menace!' called Mr Thomas, and slammed the window shut.

'Come on, Woofer,' said Mr Brown. 'You'd better come inside.'

He untied me, and I was inside the house before he'd even straightened up.

And I've slept inside the house ever since. In Woofer's corner where I belong. By nature I'm an adventurous dog, always ready for new experiences – as I proved by my readiness to accept the new kennel even with its underdog smell. And I don't mind surprises. I was really happy when Mr Brown surprised me by bringing the kennel home and setting it up in the garden. But in spite of my love for adventure and surprises, one has to draw the line somewhere, and I draw the line at change. If I'm used to something, I don't want it changed. And I'm used to Woofer's corner. I think Mr and Mrs Brown have finally got that message. I heard Mrs Brown ask Mr Brown the other day when he was going to put the advertisement in the newspaper. I think they want to sell my kennel.

6
The Wallet

Mr Brown had lost his wallet. Mr Brown often loses things. I remember him losing keys, money, books, papers, letters, lists, and his trousers, but this was the first time he'd lost his wallet.

'And there's my money and my bank card and my driving licence in it!' he cried.

'Have you got your name and address in it?' asked Mrs Brown.

'Yes,' said Mr Brown, 'but I don't need them. I can remember them.'

'In case somebody finds it,' said Mrs Brown.

'Ah!' said Mr Brown.

It was not difficult to work out how Mr Brown had lost his wallet. I'd taken him out for a walk, and as it had been a hot and sunny afternoon, he'd removed his jacket and carried it over his arm. So his wallet could have fallen out in our street, the next street, the street after that, the bookshop (where he'd popped in for a paperback), The Dog and Duck (where he'd popped in for a pint), or the park.

Phone calls to the bookshop and The Dog and Duck proved walletless, and a call to the police station had the same result.

'Come on, Woofer,' said Mr Brown. 'Let's see if we can find it.'

He then said 'Wallet' to me several times, drew a picture of a wallet, made me smell his jacket, and finally said 'Come on' again. When we were outside, he went through it once more: waving his picture and his jacket at me, and repeating 'Wallet, Woofer, wallet!' I don't know why. All we had to do was follow my own scent or his.

Anyway, I looked up at him, gave him a sympathetic wuff, and lowered my nose to the pavement.

'Good boy, Woofer,' he said.

It doesn't cost all that much to give

someone a bit of pleasure.

It was when we got near the park that I suddenly picked up a really interesting scent. In fact, no scent could have been more interesting than the one I picked up near the park. It wafted into my nose, went tingling down my backbone, and set my tail wagging like a windscreen wiper. It was the scent of Honey. Honey is the beautiful lady dog that lives four doors away, and for me to pick up her scent was like . . . well . . . Mr Brown picking up his lost wallet.

I gave a woof of excitement, and tugged Mr Brown along as fast as I could.

'Found it, eh, Woofer?' he said. 'Found the trail, eh?'

I certainly had.

Into the park we went, across the grass, into the rockery ('I don't remember us coming here,' said Mr Brown) . . . and there she was, standing next to a rosebush. And even from a distance, the rosebush couldn't compete. What fragrance, what beauty, what two-eyed, two-eared, four-

legged perfection! Should I . . . would I
. . . could I dare to speak to her?

'Hullo, Mrs Montague,' said Mr Brown.

'Oh, hello, Mr Brown,' said a voice from
somewhere in the clouds.

'Nice evening,' said Mr Brown.

'Absolutely splendid, isn't it?' said Mrs
Montague.

'Um . . . hullo, Honey,' I said.

It needs supercourage to plunge into a
conversation like that.

'Ugh,' said Honey.

Well, it was a start.

I couldn't think of anything else to say for
the moment, and somehow Mrs Montague's legs kept getting in between me and
my true love. Perhaps it was just as well. If
I'd come really close, a noseful of that scent
would have turned me into a raspberry
jelly.

Being a superdog, I'm never short of
words for long. I quickly thought up a
clever piece of conversation:

'Nice evening,' I said.

'It was till you came along,' she said.

I wasn't quite sure what she meant by that, but I pretended to laugh: 'Ha, ha,' I said. 'I like a dog with a sense of humour.'

'Who's laughing?' she said.

'Um . . . oh . . . well . . . um . . . I am,' I said.

She turned her head away, so that I could admire her sleek, truly classical profile. What a forehead! What a nose! If only I could say something, do something to impress her. It would have to be something really special, something she'd never heard or seen before, something that would make her realise that she was talking to a dog that was just as extraordinary in his own way as she was in hers.

'Oh!' Mrs Montague was saying, 'how absolutely dreadful! Fancy losing one's wallet . . .'

'Aha!' I said. 'You'll never guess what we're doing here, Honey.'

'Who cares?' she replied.

'Something really rather extraordinary,'

I said. 'I'll bet you can't guess.'

'He's lost his wallet,' she said.

'Oh!' I groaned. 'How did you know?'

'Because he's just told her,' she said.

It was the longest conversation we'd had since our unforgettable first meeting, when I'd so impressed her with the speed of my escape from the black and white tom-cat. Now I must keep it going, keep impressing her.

'What's amazing, though,' I said, 'what's really fantastic and extraordinary is . . . um . . . he lost it . . . well, um . . . when I took him out this afternoon.'

She looked straight at me. Yes, those round pools of liver-and-onion brown turned their gaze on me and me alone in this world that was suddenly empty of all other creatures.

'So what?' she said.

'Well,' I said. 'Um . . . well.'

I must admit, it wasn't a very impressive reply.

'Anyway,' said Mrs Montague, 'we'll keep our eyes peeled for it, won't we, Honey?'

She and Mr Brown said goodbye, and without even looking at me, Honey began to move away. If I didn't find something now to make her admire me, I never would. If only a savage wasp, or fly, or spider would attack her, then I could rush to her rescue . . .

'Come on, Woofer,' said Mr Brown. 'Wallet, boy, wallet.'

That was it! My only hope! Without even thinking I yelled:

'I've found it! Honey, I've found it!'

She turned round, and once again she only had eyes for me – the hero of the park.

'Where is it?' she asked.

I suppose I ought to have expected that question.

'Um . . . where's what?' I asked.

'The wallet,' she said.

'Oh,' I said. 'Um . . . well . . . no, not the wallet . . . it's not exactly the wallet . . . it's um . . . this blade of grass. It's a special blade of grass . . .'

'Come along, Honey,' said Mrs Montague.

'Come on, Woofer,' said Mr Brown.

'Goodbye, Honey!' I called. 'It was nice talking to you!'

But she didn't hear.

'Wallet, boy, wallet,' said Mr Brown.

We didn't find the wallet. It wasn't surprising that we didn't find the wallet. When we got home, Mrs Brown was waiting for us, and she was holding the wallet in her hand.

'Where was it?' asked Mr Brown in amazement.

'In your other jacket,' said Mrs Brown.

I suppose all in all it hadn't been one of my most successful adventures. But still, the wallet had been found, and I'm sure Honey had been impressed by the way I'd kept the conversation going. She'd also looked at me three times, which might have been a record. I don't think there can be many dogs that Honey would look at three times. But I don't think she can have met many dogs like me.

7
The Circus

I've always been a great entertainer. It's a matter of personality, I suppose – the extra something that makes heads turn, hands clap, and Woofer into Superdog. I wish Honey realised what a great personality I have, but maybe she's just not used to greatness.

I showed my talent at a very early age, when I appeared in a circus. I wasn't supposed to appear in the circus, because I'd been left in the car on my own, but when I started woofing and whimpering (I hate being left on my own), a couple of kind children came along and let me out.

There was a big tent nearby with jolly music coming from it, and it was obvious to my superbrain that that was where the Browns would be. And where the Browns are, you ought to find good old Woofer. So off I trotted towards the big tent.

I squeezed under the canvas, and found myself standing underneath some huge wooden steps that were joined together by hundreds of backs, bottoms and legs. It didn't take me long to work out that these were people sitting on seats, but not even I could work out which backs, bottoms and legs belonged to the Browns.

'Oompah, oompah, tiddly-idly-oompah!' went the band, and suddenly everyone was laughing and clapping. They couldn't have been clapping me, unless they had eyes in their bottoms, and so I trotted round to see what was going on.

The laughing and clapping stopped, and the music changed to 'Tiddly-idly, tiddly-idly, tiddly-idly oomp.' Then a voice boomed out: 'Now a warm welcome, please, for The Bouncing Barkers.' There was more clapping, followed by a sound that made me stand as still as a lamp-post. I could hardly believe it. The sound was a puppy-like wuff-wuffing, very high-pitched but unmistakably doggy.

It came from beyond the front seats, so I pushed through some legs, and found myself looking over a board at a big circle with people sitting all round it. Inside the circle was a woman in shiny clothes, and running round her were a dozen tiny dogs. They were as unsuper as any dogs could be, and they had different coloured ribbons and bows round their necks. If I'd looked like them, I'd have hidden away in a corner and died of shame. But there they were, in full view, all jumping up and down at the same time, wuff-wuffing and silly bows flopping. And everybody clapped! What there was to clap I really couldn't see.

I noticed that the woman slipped something into one or two of the puppy mouths. Not just applause, but food as well – and all for nothing!

There were some tubes and fences round the circle, and the next thing the toy wuffers did was run through the tubes and over the fences. More applause, more mouthfuls. It was ridiculous. Why should I sit there and let these little ribboned bow-wows get all the glory and all the mouthfuls while mighty Superdog got nothing?

The shiny woman had her back to me when I dashed out into the circle. I leapt straight over the first fence . . . well, not quite over. It was fairly high, and unluckily my hind legs caught the top of it, bringing the fence and me crashing just a little clumsily to the ground. But I was on my feet in a flash and racing through the first tube . . . well, not quite through. I got my head in, but I couldn't get the rest of me in. And I couldn't get my head out. It wasn't a very nice feeling, I can tell you.

I tried to shake the tube off, but it was stuck, and then I suppose I got into what might be called a bit of a panic. I went rushing around, leaping and waggling and bucking, and through the other end of that tube I kept catching sight of lots of faces that were all grinning. And I could hear

loud laughter and applause, though I really couldn't see what there was to laugh at.

Suddenly someone had grabbed me by the collar, and fingers appeared at the other end of the tube. One painful jerk, and it was off. More applause. I was looking into the not-very-friendly face of a man in a black suit. The shiny woman was just saying to him: 'Get that creature out of here,' and I felt his grip tighten on my collar.

'We'll soon get rid of you,' he said to me, and I certainly didn't like the sound of that.

He was holding me too tightly for me to get away, and I couldn't turn my head far enough to bite the collar-gripping hand. Nor could I reach high enough to bite the hand holding the tube. And so I bit his leg.

'Yow!' he yelled, and let go of my collar. I was away in a flash.

At my heels I could hear a high-pitched wuff-wuffing, and all around there was loud laughter and applause. The shiny woman and the black-suited man were shouting, and I was a bit surprised after running *away* from the black-suited man to find myself suddenly running *towards* him. He tried to grab me, but I did a superswerve, followed by a supersidestep as the shiny woman also reappeared.

'Wuff wuff, we'll get you, we'll get you!' yapped the prancing dolly-dogs. Of course, I wasn't frightened of *them*, but twelve sets of teeth, even puppy teeth, could nip a promising career in the bud, as they say. I might have shown them how a Superdog can fight, but I thought it wiser to show them how a Superdog can run.

It was quite a chase, and it ended when I noticed a gap in the boards round the ring. I did a sudden right turn that fooled them all, dodged a couple of pairs of hands, and went racing away into a dark tunnel. The last thing I heard was a thunderclap of applause. Obviously the audience had enjoyed my act.

At first I couldn't see very much in the tunnel, but at the end of it I came up against some iron bars. To my surprise and relief,

The Bouncing Barkers were no longer bouncing or barking behind me, and the shiny woman and the black-suited man were nowhere to be seen. I squeezed through the bars, looking behind me all the time to make sure I wasn't being followed, then turned to the front and found myself staring into the yellow eyes of the biggest dog I had ever seen. That dog was a Super-hyperfantastifabulous dog. In fact – as I found out a little later in life – he was really cheating, because he wasn't a dog at all. He was a lion. And behind him were half a dozen other lions. The one I was nearest to looked quite surprised to see me. Though he couldn't have been half as surprised as I was to see him.

'He . . . ha . . . hu . . . hello,' I said. I'm pretty good at making conversation.

The lion opened his mouth. He had teeth as long as my leg and as sharp as Mrs Brown's fingernails. I've never seen teeth like those before, and I hope I shall never see them again. Just one of his teeth could

have been cut up to give me a full set of dentures. Teeth like those shouldn't be allowed. I still have nightmares thinking about those teeth.

I don't know whether the lion had opened his mouth to yawn, to see what I tasted like, or to say hello. I didn't stay to find out. I went back through those bars, down that tunnel, through the gap in the boards and out into the circle faster than you can say he-e-elp.

I was greeted by a roar from the crowd. They know a great entertainer when they see one. But at that particular moment I wasn't thinking of entertaining them. I wasn't thinking of anything except getting out of that tent, and I raced across the ring hardly even noticing where I was heading. Just at the last moment I realised that I was going straight towards the shiny lady, and high in the air she was holding a wooden hoop. As so often before, it was my instincts that guided me, and without even thinking I took off in a mighty leap and sailed through the hoop. Well, not quite through. My head and my front legs went through. The rest of me didn't make it.

For what seemed rather a long time, I dangled over that wretched hoop, with my hind legs swinging backwards and forwards like part of a clock. Then the shiny woman waggled the hoop and I fell off. I'm sure that she and her twelve puppet-dogs and the black-suited man and the audience were amazed by the rest of my performance. In fact, I know the audience were, because they stood and cheered as I hurtled out of the circle, between two pairs of legs, under the seats, under the canvas, and out into the open field.

I didn't stop running until I reached our car, and as I couldn't get in, I got under. And I stayed under. One advantage of being smaller than a lion is that you can go where lions can't.

The Browns were quite surprised to find me under the car.

'How on earth did you get under there?' asked Mrs Brown.

I crept out, and Tina picked me up and carried me into the back seat.

'It *was* Woofer!' she said. 'I know it was.'

'It can't have been,' said Mr Brown. 'He was in the car.'

'He wasn't,' said Tony. 'He was under it.'

'*Was* it you, Woofer?' asked Mrs Brown.

Since there is only one Superdog in our family, who else could it have been? But sometimes Mr and Mrs Brown are just a little like Honey – they don't recognise greatness when they see it.

8
The Peacemaker

I am a dog of peace. Perhaps this will surprise you when you look back on some of my adventures – you will recall my reckless courage in entering the lions' cage, or in tackling the monster outside my kennel. But if I can avoid trouble, I will. Just think of the clever methods I have used to avoid trouble with the vicious black and white enemy next door.

One of my proudest moments came when I succeeded in bringing peace to the Brown family. It happened the day after we had had visitors. They had been a family just like the Browns, except for the huge difference that they hadn't got a superdog. But then, how many families have? There had been two children, and each of them had given a present to Tony and Tina. Now

Tina and I were sitting on the lawn looking at her present. Or rather I was looking at it, and Tina was eating it. The present was a bag of sweets.

'It's no use you looking like that, Woofer,' said Tina, reading my mind through my eyes. 'Mummy says you can't have any, 'cos you might choke.'

I really didn't see why I should choke on a sweet any more than I would choke on a bone, a piece of meat, or a tin of liver and onions. I said so to Tina, but the reply was simply: 'We'd better do as Mummy says.'

Tina was about a third of the way through her bag when Tony came into the garden.

'Hey!' he shouted. 'Those are my sweets!'

'No, they're not,' said Tina, 'they're mine!'

'They're not,' said Tony. 'Mark gave them to *me*!'

Tony tried to grab the bag, but Tina held on to it and smacked Tony's hand. At the second attempt Tony managed to get a grip, and as Tina still wouldn't let go, there was a loud tearing sound and the sweets spilled all over the grass.

'Now look what you've done to my sweets!' wailed Tina.

'They're not your sweets!' cried Tony. 'They're mine!'

Both of them started picking up as many as they could.

'All those are mine!' wailed Tina.

'They're mine!' cried Tony. 'And all those are mine, too!'

Then Tony tried to get hold of Tina's pile, and Tina tried to get hold of Tony's pile. Tony is bigger and stronger than Tina – just as I'm bigger and stronger than the tom-cat next door – but Tina makes up for her lack of strength by having extra sharp nails and teeth – which I suspect would be the case with the tom-cat.

I sat on the grass for a moment or two watching the fight. Then suddenly an idea came into my head. It was a memory from the previous day, and without a moment's hesitation I raced back to the house.

'Hello, Woofer,' said Mrs Brown as I bounded into the kitchen.

I gave her a wuff and a snuffle, the wuff meaning hello and the snuffle meaning I'm-perfectly-capable-of-eating-sweets-without-choking. Then I was off into the hall, on to the stairs, across the landing, and into Tony's room.

But there was no sign of what I was looking for. Could I have been wrong? I walked across the landing and into Tina's room, but there was nothing there either. So could I have been right? Back I went to Tony's room. Think, Woofer, think. Sniff, Woofer, sniff. A thorough sniff here . . . a thorough sniff there . . . a thorough sn . . . aha! . . . what's that coming from the toy box? . . . That smells like . . . let's get it open . . . it certainly smells like . . . up with the lid . . . it's the unmistakable smell of . . . ouch! (That was the toy box lid coming down on my head) . . . up again

. . . right up . . . and . . . yes indeed, the unmistakable smell and sight of one bag of sweets.

Balancing the toy box lid on my mighty shoulders, I reached down, grasped the bag in my powerful jaws, and eased my way back and out of the box. Superdogs, you see, have supermemories. The children had been given identical bags of sweets, but they hadn't seen each other's and so Tony thought that Tina had taken his. Only good old Woofer knew the full story. I would simply carry the second bag out into the garden, and the world would be at peace again.

I trotted confidently down the stairs, with the bag of sweets bumping against my chin, and I could already see the looks of surprise and I could hear the voices saying: 'Well done, Woofer. Thank you, Woofer. You'd better have some of these yourself, Woofer.' But when I reached the bottom of the stairs, the only voice I did hear was Mr Brown's, and he was saying: 'What have you got there, Woofer? SWEETS? Where on earth have you pinched them from?'

Before I knew what was happening, he'd bent down, pulled my jaws open, and taken the packet away. I wuff-whine-growled at him to give them back to me, but he had that intelligent look in his eyes which he always has when he's getting things totally wrong.

'You're a very bad dog,' he began, wagging his forefinger as if it were a tail. 'You mustn't go into people's rooms stealing things. Very naughty. You understand?'

I understood. He was the one that didn't understand. I tried to explain to him that the sweets were Tony's etc. etc., but I might as well have explained it to a buried bone. I've always had the same problem with Mr Brown. I have a similar problem with Mrs Brown.

'Naughty!' he kept saying. 'Naughty dog. Naughty to steal things . . .'

At that moment we both heard loud waulings from the kitchen.

'Now what's that?' asked Mr Brown.

Even I knew straight away that that was loud waulings from the kitchen.

'They're mine!' wauled Tina.

'They're not! They're mine!' wauled Tony.

'I don't know whose they are,' came Mrs Brown's voice, 'but you shouldn't be fighting over them.'

Mr Brown strode into the kitchen, and I followed.

'What's the matter?' he asked.

'Tony's trying to steal my sweets!'

'Tina's trying to steal my sweets!'

'They were fighting over . . .'

'Oh look!'

'Oh look!'

'My sweets!'

'My sweets!'

The voices all spoke together, and the conversation finished with Tina and Tony both pointing at the bag of sweets in Mr Brown's hand. The bag of sweets that should have been in my mouth.

They finally worked it out that Tony and Tina had been fighting over Tina's sweets, and Mr Brown was holding Tony's sweets. Then Mr Brown remembered that I was the one who'd brought Tony's sweets down, Tony and Tina remembered that I'd seen them fighting in the garden, and Tina – who is by far the cleverest member of the family – explained to the not-so-clever members of the family that obviously Woofer was the real hero of the story.

'Well fancy that!' said Mrs Brown. 'Who'd have thought our Woofer could be so clever!'

She gave me a hug and a pat. Mrs Brown is quite intelligent sometimes.

'Well done, Woofer,' said Mr Brown. 'Sorry I told you off like that.'

He patted my head and ruffled my neck.

Even Mr Brown has his bright moments.

The story did have a slightly unfortunate twist at the end, though. Tony, Tina and I went out into the garden again, with the two lots of sweets, and Tony was so pleased with me that he gave me a toffee. And in my excitement I tried to swallow it. Only it got stuck in my throat, and I very nearly choked.

9
My Bravest Deed

I have saved this story till last, because it is one of such extraordinary courage that nothing can possibly follow it. Even now I'm amazed at what I did, and my knees start shaking at the thought of what might have been done to me. Of course, now that you know me, you probably expect me to perform remarkable deeds. But I know me better than you do, and not even I expected me to perform a deed like this one.

Let me set the scene for you. We are in the market. Mrs Brown goes to the market once a week, and today she has taken Tony, Tina and me with her. Actually, I don't like the market, because there are always crowds of people, and crowds of people are not too particular what they tread on. They usually tread on me.

Anyway, there we were, three of us getting pushed and trodden on while Mrs Brown peeped, peered, poked and prodded at this and that. The stalls were set out in long rows, and the people (and I) walked in the space between, which was rather narrow. One other fact is important: next to the market is the cattle market. Though with the herds of people bleating, mooing and braying, there wasn't really much difference between the market and the cattle market.

We had stopped at a stall – or rather Mrs Brown had stopped at a stall, and the rest of us had stopped at Mrs Brown. Tony was saying he could do with an ice-cream, and Tina was saying she could do with an ice-cream as well, and Mrs Brown was saying nothing. She was poking a peach.

Suddenly, from the top end of our row of stalls, came an explosion of shouts and shrieks that even Mrs Brown had to listen to. Something terrible was happening up there, and a few seconds later we saw what it was. Ahead of us, people jumped, fell or crawled up against the stalls, making way for the thundering legs and the huge bouncy body of a runaway cow. Even at a distance it was massive, but as it galloped nearer and nearer, it seemed to swell and swell till it blotted out the whole of the rest of the world.

Mrs Brown had grabbed hold of Tina and Tony and pulled them to one side. But Tina had let go of my lead, so who was left directly in the path of the cow? That's right, Superdog, about to become Supersquash. There I stood, right in the middle of the narrow lane, with this mountain of horny bone and flesh pounding towards me.

I could tell you that my thoughts at that moment were as follows: 'This cow is dangerous. It might kill Tina and Tony and Mrs Brown and all these other people. It must be stopped.' That's what I could tell you. But I have to be honest. My thoughts at that moment were: 'This cow is dangerous. It might kill me. I wish someone would stop it.' I didn't actually think of stopping it myself. I didn't even think of jumping to one side, as everyone else had done. The fact is, I was so terrified that I couldn't even move.

You may be shocked to hear that your hero knows what it is to be afraid. But I always say there's no courage without fear. I'm not quite sure what I mean when I say that, but I must be right.

There are some instincts, however, that are even stronger than fear, and it is here that the superdog differs from the ordinary dog. I allowed my instincts to take charge, and my instincts instinctively did the right thing. So what did I do? I'll tell you.

I barked. How I barked I don't know, because my brain had gone so numb that it had totally lost touch with the rest of me. I didn't even hear myself barking. It was only when time had gone by, and I realised that I hadn't been pounded into dog-dust, that the noise of barking reached my ears. And when I finally worked out that the barking was coming from me, I guessed that I had started barking before I actually heard myself barking.

It must have been an amazing bark. Behind that bark was all the awesome power and authority of the superwonderhyperdog I had become. For when at last I opened my eyes, there in front of me, as massive but as motionless as a building, stood the cow.

'Woof woof!' I was saying. 'Wow wow wuff wuff woof woof wow wow!'

It was all quite meaningless, but the cow stood there looking at me with an expression of bewilderment on its face. And not just bewilderment either. That cow was scared. I know fear when I see it – I've felt it enough times myself to know all the signs – and that cow was looking at me with fear in her eyes.

The sight of that cow gave me a feeling of confidence. I took a step forward. And the cow took a step backward. That made me feel even more confident.

'You great stupid cow,' I said, 'what do

you mean by charging at me like that? Eh? What? Who do you think you are?'

I don't know if she understood what I said. I didn't really care.

'Just because you're as big as a house,' I said, beginning to enjoy myself, 'you think you can throw your weight around and everyone'll make way. Eh? Now, get back. Go on, get back!'

I advanced another step. And the cow retreated another step.

This was good fun. I noticed out of the corner of my eye that people were straightening up and moving a little closer to us, and I heard out of the corner of my ear that the shouting and screaming had now stopped.

'You terrified all these good people,' I said to the cow, 'and if it hadn't been for me barking at you, you could have killed somebody. You could even have killed me.'

I could happily have gone on all day telling the cow what I thought of her, but just then a tweed-jacketed, wellington-booted man puffed up behind her.

'You'm a naughty girl, Betsy!' said the booted man to the cow. 'Now calm down an' come along 'a me.'

'Naughty girl is putting it mildly!' I commented, and was pleased to see that the cow paid more attention to me than to the booted man. 'You're an absolute disgrace!'

And now voices rang out from all sides, saying things like:

'Someone could have been killed.'

'You should keep that cow under control.'

'If it hadn't been for the dog . . .'

'That dog is a hero!'

'Three cheers for the dog!'

I was very interested in what they were all saying, and while I was listening, the booted man took the opportunity to turn Betsy round and walk slowly back in the direction they'd come from.

'And don't you come charging at me again!' I called out after them. 'Or next time I'll bite your udder off!'

I saw her tail twitch and her udder shudder. That cow had had a lesson she wouldn't forget in a hurry.

From that moment onwards, I was the centre of attention. Do you remember the applause and the cheers that greeted my performance in the circus? Well, that was just a sip in the bowl compared with the worship that took place after the cow had gone.

'Ought to get a medal!' people were saying.

'Never seen such courage!'

'What a brave dog!'

'Certainly saved my life!'

'Bravest thing I ever saw!'

If only Honey had seen me that day. If only the whole world had seen me. Well, at least there's a picture of me for the whole world to see. You should study that picture carefully, because it's not every day you get the chance to see a Superhero. Look at the power of the muscles, and the intelligence of the eyes.

Mind you, when I look at myself I still marvel that such a small dog could stop such a giant cow in full flight. I wonder what I would do if the same thing happened again today. Would I stand there again and bark, and risk getting kicked up to heaven?

Well, being a superdog I expect I would do something unexpected. I'm always giving myself surprises. And if I look carefully at that picture of myself in the market, just after my bravest deed, I'm not at all certain that my expression there isn't one of surprise. In fact, it looks almost like one of shock. But that just proves what I was saying, doesn't it? Even my expression is surprising. That's the great thing about us superdogs – nobody ever knows what we'll be up to next. Not even me.